A Decision Is Yours Book

FIRST DAY BLUES

By Peggy King Anderson

Illustrated by
Rebekah J.
Strecker

LC 91-67808
ISBN 0-943990-72-6 Paper
ISBN 0-943990-73-4 Library Binding

Copyright © 1992, Parenting Press, Inc.
Published by:
Parenting Press, Inc.
P.O. Box 75267
Seattle, WA 98125

BEFORE YOU BEGIN

Most books you read tell you about other people's decisions.

This book is different! *You* make the decisions. *You* decide what happens next.

Have you ever made a decision and found things didn't turn out the way you planned? It happens all the time. Did you ever dream about going back and trying again? What would have happened if you had done something differently?

In this book you'll find out how it feels when you have to move and start at a new school. You'll have lots of chances to choose different ways of acting. You make the decisions. Good luck!

Turn the page and see what happens.

This is the first night in your new house, and **1** you feel awful. Tomorrow you have to go to a new school. Your mom pre-registered you, but you won't know anybody in this new fifth-grade class. What if you can't find your classroom?

Across the room from you, in her bed, is your bossy thirteen-year-old step-sister Stephanie. In your old house she had her *own* room.

You sigh, toss and turn, and try to get to sleep. You look over to the corner of your room and see that Ignatius, your pet iguana, is sound asleep up on his shelf.

All of a sudden you hear a noise outside your bedroom window. There it is again! It's a scratching noise, like someone's fingernails against your window. Maybe it's just the wind. But what if someone's trying to get in?

Your parents' bedroom is so far down the hall they wouldn't hear you if you called. You look over at your step-sister. Should you wake her up? You stare at the window, but you can't see anything. It's too dark. Maybe you should just pull the covers over your head and try to go to sleep.

Oh no—there it is again!

If you decide to wake your sister, turn to page 3.

If you decide to pull the covers over your head, turn to page 6.

You creep out of bed. "Stephanie!" you whisper.

She mumbles and rolls over. You shake her. "There's something at our window."

Now you can see a shadow moving back and forth by the window. "Stephanie, quick! It's trying to get in."

She groans and opens her eyes. "Megan, you have the biggest imagination of anyone I know. It's probably just the wind." She looks, then stomps over to the window. She glares at you. "It's a rosebush!"

You follow her over. Sure enough, it's the tallest rosebush you've ever seen, and the branches are scratching against the window.

You feel really dumb. Stephanie sighs. "It's okay, Megan. I remember when we moved one time when I was little. I thought I heard an elephant climbing up the stairs to get me, but it was just the furnace banging. Go to sleep."

Turn to page 4.

4   When you wake up the next morning, Stephanie is already dressed and gone, and then you remember—your first day at the new school! All of the sudden, your stomach doesn't feel so good. You go into the kitchen for breakfast and Mom puts two pancakes on your plate. "I can't eat anything," you say, "I'm too nervous."

"I know first days are hard," Mom says. "But you need to eat *something*, Megan. You'll start feeling sick if you don't. How about some juice or a piece of toast?"

If you decide to eat something, turn to page 19.

If you decide you can't eat anything, turn to page 27.

6   You pull your covers up over your head. You feel around for the flashlight that you keep handy for reading late at night. You grab the book you've hidden under your pillow and turn the flashlight on under the covers. Oh no!

The Secret of the Haunted House. Why couldn't you have hidden a different book tonight? You shove the book back under your pillow and finally fall into a restless sleep.

The next morning, you feel tired and grumpy. You get up and look out your window. There's a giant rosebush. Just then the wind comes up, and one long branch brushes against your window, making a scratching sound. So that's what that noise was!

You go to the closet to get your favorite shirt for this scary first day at your new school. It's gone! Your step-sister must be wearing it, and she's already at breakfast.

If you decide to tell Stephanie you want the shirt back, turn to page 7.

If you decide to wear something else instead, turn to page 12.

You go stomping into the kitchen. Stephanie is eating pancakes and talking excitedly to Mom. She already has a new friend to walk with her to school this morning. She met her yesterday, just walking to the store.

It isn't fair! Stephanie always makes new friends quickly. And now she's wearing *your* shirt! "Stephanie, that's my shirt and I want it back right now," you say.

"Oh, come on, Megan. It looks so good with my hair. Want to wear my denim shirt instead? That would look great on you."

You *would* like to wear that denim shirt. You've always loved it. "Well, okay," you agree, and get ready for school.

You decide to ride your bike. When you get to school, you realize you're almost late. You hurry to lock your bike at the bike rack. You don't notice the kid standing right behind you, and as you turn around you knock over his bike, and then he falls too. "Hey!" he yells. "Watch it!"

You're so embarrassed you don't know what to do.

If you apologize and help him with his bike, turn to page 9.

If you rush off, turn to page 10.

For a minute, you can't seem to get a word out.
The boy looks really mad. His face is red and his hair is sticking up all over. You swallow hard.

"Um...sorry," you say. "I guess I don't know my own strength today."

You pick up his bike. He looks at you for a minute, then bursts out laughing. "I guess you don't," he says, getting to his feet. "You new here?"

You nod.

"I'm Terry Jackson. Do you know which class you're in?"

You shake your head.

"Okay," he says, "let's get the bikes locked and I'll take you to the office."

You feel a lot better than you did a few minutes ago. At least now you've got one almost-friend—and someone to show you where to go next. You're *really* glad you stayed to apologize to Terry!

The End

10   The boy's hair is sticking up in all directions and he looks furious. Hurriedly you finish locking your bike, and rush off.

"Hey!" the boy yells again. But you ignore him. When you get into the school building, you realize you left the sheet with your class assignment in your bike bag. There's no way you want to go back and risk seeing the boy you knocked over, so you wander around the building, looking for the office. When you turn the corner, there he is. He glares at you and walks on by.

Your cheeks flush red. Oh what an awful day. If only you could have stayed in bed!

The End

12 You're so grumpy. You know you'll just start a fight with your step-sister if you go ask her about it. You get out your next best top and put that on instead. It looks okay, but you feel really mad at Stephanie for taking your shirt without asking.

When you go to breakfast, she's sitting there with *your* shirt on, eating toast, and looking happy.

You glare at her and slam a piece of toast on your plate. "What makes you so cheerful this morning?" she asks.

"You know darn good and well," you say.

"Well, I better get going," she says, getting up from the table. "I promised Julie I'd stop by on my way to school and get her."

She breezes out the door and you're left sitting there, feeling grumpier than ever.

"What's wrong?" Mom asks, as she walks over to the table with a pitcher of orange juice.

Turn to page 13.

"I'm really mad at Stephanie," you say. "She took my new shirt without asking, and I was going to wear it."

"You should have said something," Mom says. "I would have made her give it back to you."

You shrug your shoulders. "I just didn't want to start a big fight." You feel tears in your eyes and blink them back. "It's not fair that she already has a friend to walk to school with, and I don't!"

Mom comes over and gives you a big hug. "I know first days are hard, honey. Do you want me to drive you? I could go in with you to meet your teacher."

If you decide to walk, turn to page 15.

If you decide to let Mom take you, turn to page 51.

"I think I'd rather walk," you say. "I'd feel like **15** a baby, having you drive me."

"All right. I'll see you this afternoon. I'll have a special treat for your after school snack."

Mom gives you a hug, and you start off walking. It's just a few blocks, but you feel dumb walking by yourself. All around, other kids are walking in friendly groups talking.

When you get to school, you find the classroom easily and go in and sit down. Nobody talks to you, but your new teacher seems nice. She introduces you to the class, and several people smile.

The first subject for the day is math. Your teacher starts talking about factor trees and exponents.

You wonder what is she talking about. You didn't have this in your old class.

After a few minutes explanation, she passes out a worksheet and everyone gets to work. You look at it, and it might as well be in another language.

You don't understand any of this!

If you decide to go up to the teacher and tell her you don't understand the work, turn to page 16.

If you decide to try to fake it, turn to page 50.

16   You feel really self conscious as you walk up to the desk. "Ms. Fleming," you whisper. "I don't understand any of this. We never had this stuff where I went to school before."

"Oh, Megan," she says. "I'm sorry. I wasn't thinking." She pulls up a chair and quietly goes over the basics of factor trees and exponents. It's not so bad when she explains it to you one-on-one.

The recess bell rings before she finishes explaining.

Ms. Fleming looks up. "Laura, could you come up here?" The rest of the class goes out for recess and a friendly-looking girl with freckles and dark hair comes up to the desk. "Could you show Megan around for the next few days?" Ms. Fleming asks.

Laura grins. "Sure." She looks like she really means it! "Do you like to play tetherball?" she asks. You nod.

"All right. Let's go!"

You feel a happy smile popping out on your face as the two of you go out to the playground together.

The End

"Okay," you say. "I guess I could handle a piece of toast." You and Mom sit at the table while you nibble on a piece of whole wheat toast. "It isn't fair," you say. "Stephanie makes new friends so fast. I don't know anybody yet, and I hate making new friends."

"I remember how I felt when I was your age, honey," your mom says. "We moved to a new house. The first day of school, they put me in a fourth grade class by mistake, instead of fifth grade, and I was so shy I didn't say a word about it. I will say one thing though. I was the smartest person in the class for one day."

You laugh. "What finally happened?"

"My mom went back with me the next day and got it straightened out. I was really embarrassed."

"Well, I'm not *that* shy. I think if they put me in the wrong class, I'd be brave enough to say something. Thanks, Mom. I feel a little better now."

Turn to page 21.

Mom hugs you. "Here's the paper with your classroom assignment. See you after school."

You head out the door and there's Stephanie, just coming out of the house next door with her new friend, Julie. "Come on, Megan," she says. "You can walk with us until we get to the turn off for the junior high."

You walk just a little way when you see two girls laughing up ahead of you. "I know them," Julie says. "They're in fifth grade at your school, Megan. Do you want me to introduce you to them?"

If you agree to be introduced, turn to page 22.

If you say no, turn to page 57.

"Okay," you say. But your heart is pounding. What if they don't like you? What if they think you're a dork? What if your clothes are all wrong?

Your mouth is so dry, you don't think you'll be able to talk, but you follow Julie as she hurries over to the girls. "Erin and Katie, this is Megan. She's just moved here from Arizona and she's in your grade."

"Hi," Katie says.

Erin smiles. "Want to walk with us?"

You nod, feeling relieved and bashful at the same time. At first, no one says anything, but then Erin asks, "When did you move here?"

"Last week," you say. "But we just moved into our house yesterday. We stayed in a motel for the first week."

The three of you start talking then, and you begin to relax. "Do you have any pets?" Katie asks.

You grin. "I've got Ignatius. He's my iguana."

Turn to page 25.

"An iguana!" Erin squeals. "One of those big lizards that looks like a little dragon?"

You nod.

"Wow!" Katie says. "They have one in the pet store in town, and it's awesome! Could we come over after school and see it?"

"Sure," you say.

You're feeling better now. Here you are, not even at school yet, and you've made two new friends already. Maybe living in this new town is going to be okay after all!

The End

"I can't, Mom," you say. "I feel like I'm going to throw up."

Mom sighs. "All right, honey. But I'm afraid you're going to be really hungry later."

"I'll be okay." But you don't feel okay. You get your schoolbag and leave. Halfway there, your stomach starts growling. Maybe you should have eaten after all. Then you think about school and your stomach hurts again. You just don't want to go! You dawdle along, and when you get to school, everyone has already gone in. You feel like just going back home.

If you go back home, turn to page 28.

If you decide to go into the school, turn to page 46.

28   You go back home, and when you get there, Mom is in the living room unpacking boxes. She looks surprised. "Megan! What are you doing here?"

"I was late. Everyone was already in class and I didn't know where to go."

Mom looks annoyed. "Why didn't you just go to the office? They would have helped you."

"Please, Mom," you say. "Don't make me go back today. I'll go tomorrow. I promise."

"No, Megan. It will be just as hard to go tomorrow. Come on now. Try to eat something, and I'll take you back."

You're angry, but you can tell your mom isn't going to change her mind. You eat a piece of toast and then Mom drives you back to school. You wish with all your heart that you were back in your comfortable, familiar school in Arizona. When you get to the school, Mom takes you into the office.

Turn to page 31.

The secretary is really nice. "Megan, you'll be in **31** Ms. Fleming's class. I think you'll like her." She calls to a shy-looking girl who has just brought in a stack of papers. "Are you finished with the attendance sheets, Katie?"

The girl nods.

"Good! Then Megan can go back with you to the classroom."

You're relieved that you don't have to walk in alone. Your mom gives you a quick hug and you walk back to the classroom with Katie. Neither of you say anything, but you don't feel too bad because you can tell that Katie is even shyer than you are.

Katie introduces you to Ms. Fleming. She's nice, and the morning goes okay. At lunch, though, everyone else hurries to the cafeteria, and you find yourself walking in alone. This is no fun, you think.

You see Katie sitting by herself at one table, and at another table are several kids from your class, all laughing and talking. It would be nice to sit with Katie, but maybe if you sit with the other kids you can make a whole bunch of friends at once.

If you decide to sit with Katie, turn to page 33.

If you decide to sit with the group of kids, turn to page 43.

You go over and sit down at Katie's table. **33**
"Thanks for introducing me to Ms. Fleming this morning," you say.

Katie smiles. "That's okay."

"Have you been at this school for very long?" you ask.

She shakes her head. "I just got here two weeks ago. I don't know very many kids yet."

Great. Now there are two of you who don't know anyone. Neither of you says anything for a minute. Then Katie says, "My mom is trying to get me to join a club or something. This afternoon I'm going to try out for a part in the school play."

"I don't know anything about acting," you say.

"I don't either. But my mom says when you move, it's a good time to try new things. If I don't get a part in the play, I'm going to help with scenery or make-up. Want to come with me and try out too?"

If you decide to try out for the play,
turn to page 34.

If you decide not to try out for the play,
turn to page 37.

34   "Okay," you say. "I'll do it." After school you go to the play practice. Several of the kids from your class are there and they're really friendly. You do pretty well reading your part, and you get a small part in the play. Katie does too!

Ms. Fleming is the play coordinator, and she comes up to you after practice, smiling. "I'm glad to see the two of you getting involved with the play. Would you be willing to help with costumes too?"

You both agree, and when you hurry out to the parking lot later to meet Mom, you and Katie are chattering away like two old friends.

Several of the kids whose parents are picking them up wave to you. "Bye, Katie. Bye, Megan. See you tomorrow."

You're really glad you decided to try out for the play!

The End

"No, I don't think I want to do it," you say. **37** "Maybe the next time."

Katie looks disappointed. "Oh. Okay. Well, I better get going. I promised Ms. Fleming I'd take some of the props over to the auditorium during lunch."

Katie leaves, and you sit by yourself. Almost everyone else has finished lunch and gone outside. You throw your lunch bag in the trash and wander out to the playground. A bunch of kids are playing volleyball, something that you're really good at. You stand and watch for a few minutes, but no one invites you to play.

If you decide to ask if you can join the game, turn to page 39.

If you decide not to ask, turn to page 40.

You wait a few minutes until Erin, a girl you recognize from your class, comes up to serve.

"Would it be okay if I play too?" you ask hesitantly.

"Oh, sure," Erin says. "We could use another player on our team. Can you play the net?"

You nod, and the front row shifts for you to come into the game. On the very next play the ball comes to you, and you spike it over the net, hard! This is something you're good at. The other team is unable to return the ball and your team gets a point.

"All right!" the boy next to you says. Your team is looking at you with surprise, and you feel pretty good. You play a great game all the way through, and your team wins the game.

When the bell rings, two kids come up to you and tell you what a great player you are. "Will you play with us again tomorrow?" Erin asks.

"Sure," you say. This is lots better than you expected for a first day of school. It's nice to find out that your special talents can be used, no matter where you live!

The End

40   You love to play volleyball, and you're really good at it, but you're too shy to ask if you can play too. You watch for a while longer and then wander off by yourself.   You sit on a bench, feeling lonesome. A couple of times, kids walk over by you, looking as if they might say something, but you look down.   Finally the bell rings and you trudge back into class alone.

Why do first days have to be so awful? If only you could have stayed in Arizona with all your friends.

The End

You get your courage up and go to sit down with **43** the group of kids. A girl with fiery red hair scoots over to make room for you. "Hi," she says.

"You're the new girl, aren't you? I'm Kerry. This is Matt, that's Serena, and this is Elaine." You feel confused, hearing all the names at once, but they all nod and smile at you.

"We've all just joined a riding club," Kerry says. "We had our second lesson Saturday. Do you know how to ride horseback?"

You've never ridden a horse. You're scared of them. But if you say that to these kids, they'll probably think you're dumb.

If you lie, and tell them you know how to ride, turn to page 44.

If you tell them the truth, turn to page 45.

44   "Sure," you say. "I've ridden lots of times."

"That's great!" Matt says. "You can come with us Saturday and ride. We're allowed to bring guests if we want. Maybe after you ride with us, your mom will let you join the club."

"Um... I think I have to help my mom unpack stuff Saturday," you say.

"Well, how about the *next* Saturday?" Kerry asks. They're all looking at you, and you feel yourself turning red.

"No, I don't think that will work either," you say, looking down.

There is a long silence, and then everyone starts to talk about how much fun riding was last Saturday. You don't say anything. You feel bad about lying and you don't think you'll be able to be part of this group after all.

Maybe things would have worked out better if you'd just told the truth.

The End

Your heart is pounding but you decide to tell the truth. "I've never ridden a horse before," you say.

"Hey, that's okay," Matt says. "Two weeks ago was the first time I ever rode and I was scared to death."

Kerry grins. "Me too. My mom is the one that got me to try it. I'm still a little nervous, but not like before."

"If you want, you could come with us Saturday," Matt says. "We're allowed to bring guests."

"I don't know," you say. "I'm really afraid of horses."

Kerry smiles at you. "If you don't want to ride, it's all right. But why don't you come with us and watch? Afterwards we're going out for pizza."

You feel warm and happy inside. "I'll have to check with my mom," you say. "But I think it will be okay."

You're already looking forward to Saturday!

The End

46   You're feeling nervous, but you go into the school building. Over on your right is a door with a big sign that says OFFICE. You go in.

The receptionist says, "Can I help you?"

"I'm Megan Barcott," you say. "I just moved here."

She looks puzzled. "I'll have to check. There's nothing here on the desk."

But there's another lady in the office and she walks over. "I have her papers right here. I just picked them up." She smiles at you. "So you're Megan. I'm Ms. Fleming and you'll be in my class." She seems lots nicer than your teacher at your old school.

Just then your stomach gives a loud rumble. How embarrassing!

Turn to page 49.

Ms. Fleming laughs. "If you're like I was at your age, you probably didn't eat breakfast this morning. Do you have something in your lunchbag to tide you over until lunch?"

You feel embarrassed and relieved both, as you take out the apple and muffin Mom packed for you.

Ms. Fleming's eyes are kind. "Why don't you sit down over there and eat? I have a few things to do here, and then we'll go back to the classroom together."

You sigh with relief. Your teacher seems great. Maybe the kids will be okay too!

The End

50   You look around. Everyone is writing away. This is your first day and you don't want everyone to think you're dumb. You decide to fake it. You pick up your pencil and start filling in numbers, just making it up as you go.

You know the teacher will realize you don't know what you're doing, but at least right now, no one knows.

Your stomach is hurting. You hate it when you don't know what's going on. Why, oh why, couldn't you have stayed at your other school, where there were no such things as factor trees and exponents?

The End

"Okay," you say. "I'll take a ride, but don't come in with me." Mom smiles understandingly.

You get in the car and start off to school. As you get to the corner, you see a girl struggling to carry a big box.

She lives across the street from you. You saw your mom talking with her parents yesterday. Maybe you should tell Mom, so she can stop and offer the girl a ride. But what if the girl says no? Or what if she says yes, and then you can't think of anything to say to each other? You'll feel really dumb.

You look over at Mom, but she is watching the turn signal and hasn't noticed the girl.

If you keep quiet, and don't say anything, turn to page 53.

If you suggest Mom stop and offer her a ride, turn to page 55.

You decide not to say anything. The signal changes, and Mom turns the corner. You can't resist looking back. The girl is really struggling with that box, and for a minute, you wish you'd asked your mom to stop.

But after all, this is your first day at school, and you just don't feel like taking any chances. Better to not make the first move at being friends. She might have turned down a ride and then you would really feel bad. Maybe at school someone will come up to you first and offer to be friends. At least, that's what you hope.

The End

You take a deep breath to get courage. "Mom,"
you say. "That girl on the corner lives across the street from us. Should we offer her a ride?"

Mom looks over at the girl. "Oh, my goodness," she says. "She looks like she can barely walk with that big box. Of course we'll offer her a ride."

At first the girl looks startled when Mom stops beside her, but then she recognizes you and smiles. "You're Megan, right? I met your step-sister yesterday. I'm Jessica."

"Want a ride to school?" you ask.

"I'd love it! I was wondering if I'd make it there without dropping Benjie." She gets in.

"Benjie?" you ask.

"He's my pet gerbil. I'm taking him for science class. We're studying rodents this week. Want to hold him?"

Benjie scurries up the front of your shirt, nestling under your chin. You think he's adorable. You're feeling a lot better about school now than you did an hour ago. You smile at Jessica.

The End

"No, thanks," you say. "I'd rather just walk **57** with you."

All of you walk along together. Then a friend of Julie's joins the group. Julie seems nice, but her friend is snippy. "Your sister doesn't have any friends yet?" she says to Stephanie. You pretend you don't hear her, but by the time you turn off to go to your school, you are feeling really embarrassed, and wish you hadn't tagged along.

You just don't feel like you can deal with anything else today.

But just as you start up the steps to the school, a girl, bigger than you, and tough-looking, pushes you aside and knocks down all your books.

Turn to page 59.

The Decision Is Yours Series

These are fun books that help children ages 7-11 think about social problems. Written in the "choose-your-own-ending" format, the child gets to decide what action the character will take.
$3.95 each, paper, 64 pages, illus.

Finders, Keepers?
By Elizabeth Crary
What do you do when your friend wants to take money from a wallet you found?

Bully on the Bus
By Carl Bosch
What do you do when Nick, a big kid in the fifth grade, wants to beat you up?

Making the Grade
By Carl Bosch
Help Jennifer decide what to do about a bad report card after she spends more time on the soccer field than with her homework.

First Day Blues
By Peggy King Anderson
It's your first day in a new school, how will you make friends?

Biographies for Young Children

These books tell the stories of spunky girls in history who grew up to make significant changes in our society. These picture-story books are fun and riveting for preschoolers and simple enough for an eight year old to read alone.

$5.95 each, paperback, 32 pages, illus.

Elizabeth Blackwell—the story of the first woman doctor.

Harriet Tubman—the story of the famous conductor on the Underground Railroad.

Juliette Gordon Low—the story of the founder of the Girl Scouts.

ORDER FORM

Finders, Keepers	$4.95	___
Bully on the Bus	$4.95	___
Making the Grade	$4.95	___
First Day Blues	$4.95	___

Elizabeth Blackwell	$5.95	___
Harriet Tubman	$5.95	___
Juliette Gordon Low	$5.95	___
Subtotal		_____
Shipping		_____
Tax (WA add 8.2%)		_____
Total		_____

Name _____

Address _____

City _____

State/zip _____

Order subtotal	Shipping
$ 0-$10	add 2.95
$10-$25	add 3.95
$25-$50	add 4.95

Send to: Parenting Press, Inc; P.O.Box 75267, Dept.205; Seattle, WA 98125, or phone: 1-800-992-6657 for a FREE catalog.

You're furious, and you feel embarrassed with
your books lying all over the ground and people
staring. But you take a deep breath and decide you
can deal with this.

"I must be invisible today," you say, making a
face. A couple of people chuckle.

One girl, with red hair and freckles, leans down
to help you pick up your books. "Are you new
here?" she asks.

You nod.

"I'm Kerry," she says. "Don't mind old Harriet
Stomper. She likes to push people around, just to
see them get mad."

She hands you back your entrance card. "Hey!
You're in Ms. Fleming's class. So am I. Come on,
we'll walk to class together."

You let out a relieved sigh. Maybe this awful day
will turn out all right after all! You and Katie walk
down the hall together to class.

The End